CAPTAIN PUGWASH
and the PIGWIG

JOHN RYAN

F

FRANCES LINCOLN
CHILDREN'S BOOKS

First published in 1991 by Viking

This edition published in Great Britain and the USA in 2010 by
Frances Lincoln Children's Books, 4 Torriano Mews,
Torriano Avenue, London NW5 2RZ
www.franceslincoln.com

A catalogue record for this book is available from the British Library.

ISBN 978-1-84780-025-1

Printed in Croydon, Surrey, UK by CPI Bookmarque Ltd. in January 2010

1 3 5 7 9 8 6 4 2

Contents

Captain Pugwash
and the Pigwig

One day, while strolling
through the market, Captain
Pugwash saw a fat little
suckling piglet for sale.

"That's *just* the thing to
make me a delicious dinner
when we set sail tomorrow," he
thought.

8

So he bought it, and carried
it back to his ship.

He felt very
pleased with
himself and
could hardly
wait for Tom
the cabin boy
to cook it next
evening.

9

But no
sooner had
the ship set
sail than
the piglet
escaped

from the larder and started to
make friends with the crew.

It could do all sorts of tricks.

Like sitting
up and begging
for food,

and walking
on its front
trotters,

and turning
somersaults.

11

Soon all the pirates became
very fond of the piglet. They
didn't at all want their Captain
to have it for his dinner.

"We have all become
vegetarian, Cap'n," said the
Mate. "If you try to roast that
there pig, there will be trouble,
mark my words."

"Lay one finger on 'im, and we'll throw you to the sharks and the sea monsters," growled Pirate Barnabas.

"Aye! And sharks and sea monsters are NOT vegetarian!" added Pirate Willy.

13

"Fluttering flatfish," said Pugwash. "What a fuss about a fat little piglet!"

But there was nothing he could do. The crew named their new pet "Pigwig"

and the Captain had to watch them feeding him every kind of delicacy – out of *his* larder!

Then Pigwig
started to grow.

He got bigger
and fatter,

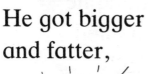

and bigger
and fatter,
until he
wasn't a piglet any more . . .

but a huge great porker!

Then the crew decided that
Pigwig needed more
comfortable quarters.

So he
had his meals at the Captain's
table,

and slept in the Captain's bunk.

Poor Captain Pugwash. There was very little room left for him, and it soon became rather smelly in his cabin.

In fact, all over the ship,

the pirates were having to hold
their noses.

Another problem was that as
Pigwig grew bigger, so did his
appetite.

The ship's food supplies were
beginning to run low –

and the crew began to wonder
whether their pet *was* such a
good thing after all.

Then Tom the
cabin boy,
who had been
keeping very
quiet, called
out, "Look!
There's an island over there!

Let's go ashore and see if
there's any food."

"Good idea, Tom lad," said
the Mate. "Man the longboat,
Shipmates!"

20

So they dropped anchor and the crew rowed ashore in the longboat.

The island was full of trees and shrubs covered with fruit and berries and nuts. Just what the pirates were looking for.

Soon they were on their
way back, with baskets full
of goodies.

Then Tom
steered the
ship far
away from
the island.

Meanwhile, Captain
Pugwash and the pirates settled
down to the biggest and best
meal they had had for a long
time. It was only when they
were beginning to feel really
full and rather sleepy that the
Mate remarked:

"That's werry peculiar! I don't see our Pigwig nowhere!"

"You're right . . . 'ee's gone!" cried Barnabas.

"Pig overboard!" called Willy, running to the side.

But Tom smiled. "Don't worry," he said. "I rowed

Pigwig ashore in the dinghy while you were looking for food.

I left him there. He's far better off with his own kind."

Tom was right. On the island, Pigwig had already met lots of interesting gentlemen pigs, and attractive lady pigs. He was very happy indeed. His new companions were much more fun than the pirates!

On board the ship the crew were happy too. In fact, they danced with joy because now there was plenty to eat . . .

and it wasn't anything like so smelly!

Only Captain Pugwash wasn't
quite as pleased as everybody
else.

After all, he had never had
that delicious dinner he had so
looked forward to at the start
of the voyage!

Captain Pugwash
and the Parrot

It was the Captain's birthday,
and his crew wanted to give
him a present.

They thought of an
eye-patch, but that reminded
them of their worst enemy,
Cut-throat Jake. They thought
of a wooden leg, but
remembered that Pugwash
already had two perfectly good
legs.

So, in the end, they decided
on a parrot.

"Every pirate should have
one," said the Mate.

"Ar . . . and they come
cheap round here," said
Barnabas.

So, as the ship was in
harbour, they went ashore and
bought the least expensive
parrot they could find.

"Happy Birthday, dear Cap'n," sang all the pirates together as they gave Pugwash his present.

"Happy Birthday!" sang the parrot . . . and bit the Captain on the nose.

"Ouch! . . .
er, yes, er,
well . . . thank
you very
much,"
said Pugwash.
He wasn't very
fond of birds, and had already
taken a strong dislike to this
one.

"I take it,"
he said,
as he stuck
a plaster on
to his nose,
"that you
have bought
a *cage* for the creature?"

"No cage, Cap'n," said the Mate.

"Money ran out," said Barnabas.

"Christmas is coming," said Willy.

34

"You'll have to keep it in your cabin, Cap'n," said the Mate,

and because he didn't want to hurt the crew's feelings, Captain Pugwash agreed.

So Tom the cabin boy, who seemed to get along quite well with the parrot, took it and made it comfortable in the Captain's cabin.

But sadly, right from the start,

the birthday present was *not* a success.

The parrot snapped at its new owner

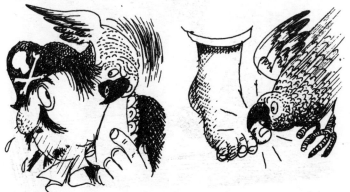

whenever Pugwash came within reach . . .

and also started to imitate the Captain in a very rude manner.

It took to repeating his favourite sayings, like "What-ho, me hearties!" or "Shuddering sharks!" or "Jumping jellyfish!".

Sometimes it shouted out orders in the Captain's voice, like "Splice the mainbrace!", which means "Free rum for all!".

This made the crew, who loved their rum, very happy, and the Captain, who was as mean as anything, very cross.

But the parrot did worse than that. Every day after lunch, the Captain liked to take a little snooze.

When he snoozed, he snored.

And when he snored, the parrot imitated his snoring.

40

He did it so cleverly that
nobody could tell the difference.

The parrot's snoring became
so loud that

the Captain couldn't sleep at
night, let alone after lunch!

One afternoon, Pugwash got fed up with trying to sleep. So he decided to take a walk into town with the crew.

Little did he realize that his enemy, Cut-throat Jake, was lurking near by and planning a raid on the *Black Pig*.

In fact, that very afternoon,
thinking that the Captain
would be asleep as usual, Jake
sneaked up the
gangplank,

across the
deck,

and along to
the Captain's
cabin.

The only person in sight was
Tom the cabin boy, and for
once Tom seemed quite
friendly.

"Looking for the Cap'n?"
Tom asked. "Listen!"

Then, with his ear to the Captain's door, Jake heard the Captain's voice.

"Battling barnacles! It's my bedtime!" said the voice, and there followed a lot of loud snoring.

"Ha-harrh! . . . asleep, eh? . . . caught like a lobster in a pot," breathed Jake.

Waving his cutlass, he rushed
into the cabin.

The Captain wasn't there, of
course . . . but the parrot was!
It took one look at the
intruder, and went for him!

Cut-throat Jake was a
savage fighter, but he was no
match for the parrot!

Pecked and scratched
and bitten, he fled in terror
out of the cabin,

off the ship,

and away down the quayside.

And that was what Captain
Pugwash and his crew saw as
they strolled back to the *Black
Pig*.

"Well, well, well," said
Pugwash, "it's that old villain,
Cut-throat Jake.

We shan't see *him* again for a
while, by the look of it!"

"Nor," he added to himself
with a happy smile,

"my birthday parrot!"

Captain Pugwash
and the Plank

It was a very very hot day. The
Black Pig was becalmed in the
Caribbean sea. The Mate,
Willy and Barnabas were lying
about on deck, snoozing and
sunbathing and doing nothing
very much.

Even Tom the cabin boy, who
usually did all the hard work,
was reading a book in a shady
corner.

Captain Pugwash wasn't
doing much either. He had just
eaten a very large lunch. Now
he was sleeping it off
peacefully in his cabin.

As he slept, the Captain began
to dream . . .

. . . and his dream was
anything but peaceful!

He dreamed that his crew were fed up with him. So much so that they had decided they didn't need a Captain any more and could run the ship by themselves.

"Help! This is mutiny!" thought Pugwash in his dream.

Worse was to come.

"Let's get rid of him altogether!" said the Mate.

"Ar!" put in Willy. "Who wants an extra mouth to feed?"

"Tell you what," chuckled Barnabas, "let's make 'im walk the plank . . . and make an end of 'im!"

Then all the pirates cheered, and even Tom, his faithful cabin boy, started to fix up the plank.

Poor Captain Pugwash! His dream was fast turning into a nightmare!

For now the pirates were
pushing him out along the
plank.

"Jump for it, Cap'n!"
shouted the
Mate. "Or
we'll blow
you off
with the
cannon!"

The Captain jumped. He fell
and he fell and he fell . . . and
he landed . . .

with a bump

. . . wide awake on the floor of
his cabin. He had fallen out of
his bunk and
woken up.

"Whew!" breathed Captain
Pugwash. "What a relief! It
was only a bad dream!"

But then he heard a noise
outside on the deck. It was a
hammering noise. It was just
like the hammering noise he
had heard in his dream, when
Tom was nailing down the
plank. So he peeped out on
deck . . .

and "OH NO!!" he
muttered.

"It's TRUE!!" For there was
Tom the cabin boy,

and he really *was* nailing a
plank to the deck! The Mate
and Barnabas stood around
watching him gleefully.

"Tottering turtles! This is truly terrible!" thought the Captain.

"There really *is* a mutiny going on! There's only one thing to do . . . escape . . . before they come for me and make me walk the plank!"

Quickly he put on his coat
and his boots. He packed a
basket full of food
and water
and a flask
of rum.

He stuffed a small treasure-
chest with all
the gold and
silver and jewels
that he kept
hidden in his
cabin.

It was quite a job to shut it
because he couldn't bear to
leave anything behind. Then
he carried everything stealthily

out of his cabin and along to
the far end of the *Black Pig*,
where the dinghy was kept.

He loaded all his precious things into the little boat, and was just about to lower it very very quietly over the side, when he heard Tom calling him.

"What on earth are you doing messing about with the dinghy?" cried the cabin boy. "We're all going to have a swim and cool off!

I've just fixed up a DIVING-BOARD! Come on!"

"Oh, there you are,
Cap'n!" called the Mate as
Pugwash and Tom arrived.
"Come and join us!"

The pirates were all
dressed in their
swimming things.

"You go first, Tom lad!"
said Barnabas. "Show us how
to do it!"

So Tom ran along the plank
and did quite a neat
swallow-dive.

He hardly
made any
splash as
he entered
the water.

Willy went next. He did a honey-pot and made quite a splash.

Barnabas tried a back-dive and made a very big splash.

The Mate did a belly-flop and made a very big splash indeed.

But Captain Pugwash did a back-front double somersault, with a special sideways twist . . . and made the biggest splash

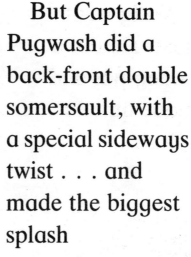

of the lot! He was so happy to find that the plank was only a diving-board after all.

He even managed to keep
his hat on!

Captain Pugwash
and the Poop Deck

"All hands to the poop deck, Master Mate!" cried Captain Pugwash. "Fluttering flounders! It's absolutely filthy up here. High time the deck was given a good scrubbing!"

"Aye, aye, Cap'n," grunted the Mate sleepily.

"Come on, look sharp,
Barnabas and Willy! All hands
to the poop
deck!"

Barnabas was fishing and
Willy was playing skittles.
Neither of them was in any
hurry to obey
the Mate's
command.

"Wot is a poop deck, anyway?" grumbled Willy, as he set to work.

"Really, Pirate William," said Captain Pugwash. "How long have you been at sea?

The poop deck is the highest deck at the stern, or back end, of the ship, of course!

On it is the steering-wheel, and there stands the most important person aboard . . . the Captain himself . . . *me*!"

"When 'ee's not asleep in 'is cabin," muttered Barnabas. But the Captain pretended not to hear.

"And," he went on, "by
far the bravest, most
handsome buccaneer . . ."
But suddenly the
Captain was rudely
interrupted.

"I'll give 'ee brave an'
'andsome!!" snarled a
ferocious voice behind him.

There, to everybody's
horror, was Cut-throat Jake,
the Captain's worst enemy.
Silently, he had climbed up the
stern of the ship.

Now he leaped over the rail, on to the deck and roared:

"Come on, you old scallywag Pugwash! Draw your sword! We'll soon see who's the bravest an' most 'andsome."

The crew were terrified. A few seconds later, there wasn't one of them to be seen. They had all slipped away from the poop  deck to a place from which they could watch

without being seen.

 Even Tom the cabin boy had disappeared, though nobody quite knew where.

But most frightened of all was Captain Pugwash.

For all his boasting, he was no good at fighting at all! He was certainly no match for Cut-throat Jake.

"Help!" cried Pugwash,

as his deadly enemy chased
him up and down the poop
deck, slashing at him with his
enormous cutlass.

In vain,
the
Captain
tried to
dodge
round
the steering-wheel.
He tried to
escape up the
rigging.

But Jake
cut him
down again.

He tried to jump over the
side, but Jake pulled him
back again.

Then he knocked the sword
out of Pugwash's
hand,

and tied him
up with his own rope.

From a safe distance, the crew watched while Cut-throat Jake strode up and down, waving his cutlass in triumph and stroking his huge black beard.

"That'll teach 'im to tell us to scrub decks," muttered Barnabas.

"Looks like we've got a new Cap'n," whispered Willy.

"Oh dear!" said the Mate.

Willy was right.

"Ha-ha-harhh!!" roared Cut-throat Jake. "The vessel is mine – all mine, an' I'll sail her to my own home port!"

And he seized the wheel with his great hairy hands and began to turn the ship.

But what Jake had not
realized was that he was
standing on a hatchway,

and that in the sail-locker
underneath,

Tom the cabin boy was busy
undoing the bolt.

Suddenly, in the middle of a
roar of triumphant laughter,
Cut-throat Jake found himself
falling through the poop deck,
into the sail-locker below.

Quick as a flash, Tom
climbed up through the
hatchway

. . . pulled it tight shut . . .

and lashed it to the base of the
steering-wheel with some rope.

Jake was imprisoned and very
uncomfortable. He swore
horribly, but there was nothing
he could do about it, and there
he stayed for the rest of the
voyage.

So the *Black Pig* continued
on her way . . .

with Captain Pugwash at the
wheel. He was even more
pleased with himself than ever.

"Poor old Cut-throat Jake," he boasted to the crew. "His wicked plots always fall through – HA HA – in the end!

And as for all of you – I hope you will always remember what a poop deck is: the place where the most important person on board is always to be found!"

"Hmm," thought Tom. "If you ask me, *our* poop deck is a place where you find silly old poops!"

But he just smiled . . . and said nothing.